Clifford
Takes a Trip

Clifford
Takes a Trip

Norman Bridwell

SCHOLASTIC INC.

New York Toronto London Auckland
Sydney Mexico City New Delhi Hong Kong

To Tracy

ISBN B-6K5-61521-1
Copyright © 1966 by Norman Bridwell.

All rights reserved. Published by Scholastic Inc.
SCHOLASTIC and associated logos are trademarks and/or registered trademarks of Scholastic Inc.
CLIFFORD, CLIFFORD THE BIG RED DOG, BE BIG, and associated logos are trademarks and/or registered trademarks of Norman Bridwell.

Library of Congress Cataloging-in-Publication Data is available.

12 11 10 9 8   18 19 20 21 22/0

Printed in Malaysia   106
This edition first printing, August 2013

Hi, I'm Emily Elizabeth.
This is a happy day for me.

This is the last day of school.
Summer vacation is here!
Now I can play with my dog, Clifford.

We don't go on long vacation trips.
It's too hard to get Clifford on a bus
or train.

We only go to places that Clifford can walk to,
like picnics in the park.

Last year was different.
Last year we went to the mountains.
Mommy and Daddy said it was too far
for Clifford to walk.

So we left him with the lady next door.

That night Clifford was so lonely
he began to howl.
He howled and he howled
and he howled —

— until someone threw a shoe at him.
It didn't hurt Clifford's nose,
but it did hurt his feelings.

The next morning Clifford set out to find us.
He sniffed his way along the road.

Clifford didn't mean to make trouble.
But a lot of people had never seen
a big red dog before.

Clifford kept going.
Nothing could stop him.

And then he saw a little old man
trying to fix his truck.
The man needed help.

So Clifford stopped and helped him.
He took the little old man to a garage.

The little old man gave Clifford a little lunch,
to thank him for his help.

Then Clifford set out again.

Nothing stopped him — not even wet cement.

And traffic jams didn't stop him.
Clifford just tiptoed over the cars.
And then . . .

... he came to a toll bridge.
Clifford had no money.

But that didn't stop him.

We didn't know Clifford was coming.

I found some new playmates —
two baby bears.
I was having so much fun
I didn't see Mama Bear.

She didn't want strangers
to play with her babies.
She growled.
I was in real trouble.

Then we heard a LOUDER growl.
Guess who was growling!

Mama Bear was surprised.

She even forgot her babies.
I told Clifford that the Mama Bear
was only protecting her children.

Good old Clifford
took the baby bears
back to Mama Bear.

Then he took us all back to camp.
Mommy and Daddy were surprised
to see Clifford.

I told them how Clifford saved my life.

So they let Clifford stay with us.

Next year, maybe we will find a way
to take Clifford with us
when we go on vacation.